Word List

Here is a list of words that might make it easier
to read this book. You'll find them in boldface
the first time they appear in the story.

wilderness	WIL-der-nuhs
endangered	in-DAYN-jerd
species	SPEE-sheez
emergencies	i-MER-juhnt-sees
description	di-SKRIP-shun
peculiar	pi-KYOOL-yer
hoax	HOHKS
binoculars	buh-NO-kyuh-lers
devoured	di-VOURD
unmistakable	uhn-muh-STAY-kuh-buhl
constellations	kon-stuh-LAY-shunz
chokecherries	CHOHK-chair-eez
tripod	TREYE-pod
papier-mâché	pay-per-muh-SHAY

Barbie™

Clawman's Warning

BARBIE and associated trademarks are owned by and used under
license from Mattel, Inc. © 1999 Mattel, Inc. All Rights Reserved.
Published by Grolier Books, a division of Grolier Enterprises, Inc.
Story by Jacqueline A. Ball. Photo crew: Tom Wolfson,
Patrick Kittel, Laura Lynch, Robert Holley, and Judy Tsuno.
Produced by Bumpy Slide Books.
Printed in the United States of America.

ISBN: 0-7172-8857-9

Morning sunlight sparkled on the snowy peaks. Barbie leaned back and took a deep breath of clean, cool air.

Barbie was on vacation at the Rocky Mountain Lodge in Johnson, Wyoming. Although it was late summer, mornings were cold in the hills. She pulled her brown vest more tightly around her.

A door opened and then banged shut. Two girls dressed in jeans and turtlenecks raced onto the wide porch. They sat on the wooden railing, swinging their legs.

"Hi, Stacie," Barbie said, getting up. She ruffled her younger sister's blond hair. "Hi, Janet. All ready for our big adventure?"

"You bet!" Stacie exclaimed. "We can't wait!"

Janet's eyes flashed with excitement. "I could hardly sleep last night! Neither could Mom."

Janet's mother, Carolyn, had come along to help Barbie look after Stacie and two of her closest friends. They were going to hike to a beautiful **wilderness** spot called Eagle Pond. On the way, they would camp overnight.

Just then the door opened. Stacie's other friend, Katie, darted out. She jumped onto a big chair and snuggled down into its cushion.

"Ask us what birds we'll see at Eagle Pond, Barbie," said Katie eagerly. A big smile lit up her face. They had been kidding around all week.

"Okay," Barbie played along. "What kind of birds live at Eagle Pond? Take a wild guess."

"Eagles!" the girls shouted.

"Right," Barbie said. "Bald eagles. That's how the lake got its name. And since bald eagles have been taken off the **endangered species** list, our chances of seeing one will be better than ever."

As Barbie spoke, a pretty woman wearing a fleece pullover joined them. Her arms were clasped across her chest. She was shivering.

"That's good news about the eagles," the woman said. "The other good news is that breakfast is ready! And *I'm* ready for some hot chocolate! It's hard to believe August can be this chilly."

"It will warm up later, Carolyn," Barbie said. "Then it will get cool all over again tonight. That's why I told the girls to wear layers of clothing. They can take off or put on what they need."

Stacie shaded her eyes and looked down the driveway. "I see a jeep," she said.

"It must be Ken," said Barbie. "I've been expecting him."

A dark green Park Service jeep stopped in the driveway. Barbie's friend Ken leapt out and trotted up to the porch. He wore a park ranger's uniform.

"Good timing," Barbie greeted him. "We were just about to go in for breakfast."

"Super!" Ken replied. "I've been behind the wheel since five o'clock, and I'm starving."

Ken was working as a Johnson Park ranger for the summer. He had spent time camping in the Rockies when he was younger, and he knew the area well. He had helped Barbie plan her trip, including the Eagle Pond hike.

He sniffed the air. "Mmmm. I smell bacon!"

The three girls jumped to their feet.

"Let's eat!" cried Janet.

"Excuse us!" said Katie.

"Please!" Stacie added.

They ran inside, slamming the door again.

4

Barbie chuckled. "I hope they save some of that energy for later. We're going to hike six miles today, mostly uphill."

Carolyn groaned and pushed open the door. "In that case, I'd better go fuel up myself."

"We'll be right in," Barbie called. She turned to Ken. "What were you doing out at five o'clock? Isn't that awfully early, even for a ranger?"

"We got a call about a missing hiker," Ken answered. "A young guy named Chris Wilson went out a few days ago. His friends haven't heard from him since. I joined the search party at dawn. But so far, there's been no trace of him."

"I hope he's not hurt," Barbie said.

"So do I," Ken agreed. "And I hope he knows as much about wilderness safety as you do, Barbie. But I doubt it."

"What was he wearing," Barbie asked, "in case we spot anything on the trail?"

"Navy blue jacket, jeans, and an orange

bandanna around his neck," replied Ken.

"I'm taking a cellular phone with me for **emergencies,**" Barbie said. "I'll call the ranger station if we find anything."

Ken lowered his voice. "I'm really glad you'll have a phone, Barbie, because there's something else . . ."

Just then, Stacie burst through the door. "Come on," she called. "Janet's mom says we should be polite and wait for you before we start eating."

"Okay, Stacie, we're coming," Barbie said.

"Let's talk later," Ken added softly.

Barbie wondered what was troubling Ken. It was clear that he didn't want to discuss it in front of Stacie.

In the dining room, a long table held rows of serving pans. Steam rose from the food inside them.

"Everything smells so good," said Barbie.

A short man with a red, windburned face was serving. He wore a white chef's apron over his cowboy shirt and jeans. He gave Barbie and Ken a friendly wave with a big spoon.

"Hey there, Randy," Ken said.

Barbie's group started down the line. Randy dished out bacon, eggs, and fried potatoes. The group helped themselves to fruit and muffins. At the table, Ken and Barbie went over wilderness safety rules. Ken repeated his **description** of the missing hiker.

When Carolyn and the girls went back for seconds, Barbie asked Ken what he had started to say earlier.

"We got this kind of disturbing report," he replied. "I'm sure you'll be in no danger, but . . ."

"More hot chocolate, folks?" offered Randy. He stood behind them, holding a pot. They nodded, and he filled their cups.

The others returned. "Barbie, how far is it to the pond?" Janet asked.

"Eight miles," Barbie answered. "We'll hike

the hardest, longest part today. Tomorrow's walk will be much shorter and easier."

"Which pond?" Randy asked. His blue eyes were bright with interest.

"Eagle Pond," Stacie told him excitedly, "where bald eagles nest."

Randy's mouth dropped open in surprise. "Eagle Pond!" he exclaimed. "Haven't you heard about the sighting there?"

"What sighting?" Carolyn asked.

Ken held his finger to his lips, warning Randy to be quiet.

Randy paid no attention to him. "Someone saw an animal up there," he answered slowly. "A real **peculiar** critter. Looks like a bear. Walks like a man. He has three claws like hooked razors on each paw. They call him . . ."

"Clawman!" the three girls shrieked.

The other guests in the dining room stopped talking. The room went silent.

Chapter Two

"Clawman?" Carolyn repeated. She looked confused. "Who's Clawman?"

"You really don't know, Mom?" asked Janet. "Everyone knows about Clawman!"

"It's not a *who,* it's a *what,*" Randy explained, pulling up a chair. He poured himself a steaming mug of hot chocolate and took a sip. "It's a thing. A thing that folks say has been roaming these hills since the Ice Age."

Barbie looked doubtful. "Come on, Randy. Everyone knows that Clawman isn't real. It's a **hoax.** A story somebody made up."

"But what about that picture?" Stacie protested. "We saw it on TV. It showed Clawman running into the woods, sort of looking over his shoulder."

"You mean the video was taken *here?*" Janet exclaimed.

"I saw the picture in a newspaper, too," added Katie excitedly. "So it must be true!"

"Experts say that picture is a fake," Ken told them. "But people still believe that Clawman is real. From time to time, someone reports seeing him, which is what happened here a couple of days ago." He turned to Barbie. "That's what I've been trying to tell you. I'm sure you're in no danger, but I didn't want to upset the girls." He frowned at Randy.

The cowboy's face turned redder. "Well, I didn't mean to upset you folks, either," Randy said quickly. "Probably no need to worry, anyway. If Clawman is up there, you'll hear him coming for miles. They say he makes a sound like this."

The cowboy puckered his lips. A strange sound somewhere between a whistle and a howl came out.

"*Woo—EEEE—ah!*"

"It sounds like a werewolf," Janet said.

"Randy, I think that's enough," Carolyn stated.

"And his smell?" Randy continued. "Hoowee, does that critter stink! Like an old tuna fish can wrapped in yesterday's gym socks."

"Ugh!" moaned Katie.

"Yuck!" cried Stacie.

"Ee-yoo!" wailed Janet.

"Now, that *is* enough," Barbie told Randy firmly. "More than enough."

But Randy wasn't quite through being helpful. "So you all remember, if you hear this sound—don't stick around!" He made the weird whistle one more time before returning to the serving table.

Stacie grabbed Katie's arm. "I'm scared!"

"What if Clawman is waiting for us on the trail?" Katie wondered.

"Or at the pond?" Janet cried. "Or where we're camping, so he can get us when we're asleep!"

"Clawman is not real," Barbie said calmly. "Anyway, even in the stories, he's described as shy and harmless. They say he eats only berries and twigs and keeps to himself."

"Randy's just trying to scare you," added Carolyn. She looked puzzled. "Although I can't imagine why. Don't take him seriously."

"Randy has been telling Clawman stories for so long, he probably believes them himself," Ken explained. "It makes him feel important."

"Well, it's important for us to be on our way," said Barbie. "We need every bit of daylight to make camp in time."

Ken unfolded a map, and the group crowded around it. Barbie pointed to spots highlighted in yellow marker. "Here's our trail," she said. "And here's Aspen Falls, where we'll camp tonight. Ken will meet us there tomorrow. Then we'll all follow this logging road to Eagle Pond."

"Near the lake, there's a fire tower with awesome views," Ken told them. "You guys can climb

up and take pictures, and I can scout out the mountainside for that hiker we've been searching for. If we haven't found him by then, that is."

"Or if Clawman hasn't gotten him by then," Stacie said.

"Or if Clawman hasn't gotten *us* by then!" Janet added, shuddering once again.

Talking in worried whispers, the girls went to their rooms and got their backpacks. They dragged the gear out to the porch. Each carried a sleeping bag, extra clothes, and a water bottle.

Barbie and Carolyn were carrying packs that

held two tents, food, a first-aid kit, and a cooking pot. Barbie also packed a small gas camping stove. To reduce the risk of forest fires, open campfires were not allowed on the trail.

As the hike began, the girls walked quietly. They crossed a meadow filled with wildflowers and humming with insects. Suddenly they heard a surprising sound.

"Was that a meow?" asked Stacie.

"I hope a cat isn't lost out here," said Janet.

Then they saw a gray bird flutter from a pine branch. It made a shrill mewing sound.

"It's not a cat, it's a bird!" exclaimed Katie.

Barbie peered through her **binoculars.** "A talented bird. It's a mockingbird. Mockingbirds mimic the sounds other birds and animals make."

"I wonder if they can imitate Clawman like Randy," said Carolyn.

"Mother!" Janet protested. But everyone laughed. The laughter helped the girls relax, and soon they were having fun on their adventure.

The ground quickly sloped upward and became a steep trail. Barbie showed the others how to follow painted marks called blazes to stay on the right path.

The sun grew brighter and hotter as they walked. The girls kept stopping to remove layers of clothing and to apply bug spray and sunblock. Even though the sun was hot, there were occasional patches of snow. One large patch caught Barbie's eye. It was marked with three-pointed clusters.

"What unusual tracks," Barbie said, kneeling. "I wonder what could have made them."

"Something with three toes?" guessed Katie.

"Or three claws," added Stacie.

"Clawman!" cried Janet.

17

Barbie stood up and flipped through her field guide. "Really, girls. I'm sure these tracks were made by something perfectly ordinary," she said. But nothing in the guide matched the tracks in the snow.

They started walking again. But now the girls were more fearful than ever. Every few minutes, they begged Barbie to check behind a rock or tree.

"Time for lunch," Barbie finally said. "Maybe food will help calm them down," she thought.

They stopped at a smooth gray rock ledge overlooking the valley. Below them they could see the Rocky Mountain Lodge, tiny as a dollhouse.

"Wow! Look how far we've climbed!" Katie exclaimed.

Carolyn pulled plastic bags out of her pack. Barbie unrolled a tarp and spread out a feast of sandwiches, fruit, and cookies. The girls were hungry from the tough workout. Before long, they had **devoured** every crumb.

"Mmmm!" Stacie said, licking her fingers. "Peanut butter and jelly never tasted so good!"

Barbie took a sip of a high-energy sports drink. She gazed down at the lodge and the surrounding cabins, fields, and barns. It was like looking at a toy world.

"What a fantastic picture that would make," Barbie thought. She took out her camera and set it on a flat rock. As she adjusted the lens, her hand brushed against something. It was a round piece of black plastic, caught in a crack in the rock. One edge was jagged, as if it had been broken.

Barbie shook her head. "Someone certainly was careless," she said. "Trash should never be left around to spoil the scenery for others."

She put the fragment into a garbage bag. "We'll throw this away back at the lodge."

The group finished lunch and began hiking again. The food put the girls in a much better mood. They walked more quickly, singing choruses of "This Old Man." Their happy voices bounced off boulders and echoed through the woods.

The trail became narrower and rougher. They tripped over loose stones and roots. Low branches whipped their faces.

Barbie suggested they walk in single file and take turns being the leader.

By the time it was her turn, Stacie was bored and impatient. "I want to see how far it is before the trail gets easier," she said, racing ahead.

"Stacie, wait!" called Barbie. "Stay with the group!"

But Stacie was already out of sight.

Then they heard her terrified scream.

"Help! It's got me by the hair!"

"Stay still, Stacie!" Barbie shouted. She edged past the others and hurried to reach her sister.

Stacie stood struggling in the middle of the trail, batting wildly at a tree above her head. Her hair was tangled in the branches.

"Calm down, Sis," Barbie said. "Your hair is caught in the tree, that's all. I'll get you free."

As she gently untangled Stacie's hair, Barbie's hand touched something soft.

"Yuck! I smell something nasty, Barbie," Stacie complained. She smoothed down her hair and added, "Like rotten fish."

The rest of the group arrived, out of breath.

"Are you okay, Stacie?" asked Katie.

"What happened?" Carolyn wondered.

"Phew! What's that stink?" cried Janet.

Barbie pulled down the soft object. She saw

that it was a big clump of reddish brown fur. Its foul smell hung in the air.

Stacie's eyes widened with fear. "Clawman!" she cried. "Clawman was here!"

"And there!" Katie gasped, pointing.

They all gazed up at another branch studded with fur clumps.

"And there," added Janet.

Clumps of the stuff were draped everywhere!

"See how trampled the ground is," Carolyn said, "as if something stomped through here."

The area was littered with broken sticks and crushed leaves. Patches of snow were stamped with the same three-pointed clusters they had seen earlier.

The girls stood back, their eyes wide.

"Let's keep calm," Barbie warned. "And, please, let's keep remembering that Clawman does not exist. Whoever did this is showing disrespect for nature and other people. I'm going to gather up these pieces, whatever they are. They could be important clues to what's going on around here."

Using a sandwich bag as a glove, Barbie carefully collected the filthy, smelly fur. She looked at it closely. Something about them was strange.

"It doesn't look like real fur," she thought. "It looks fake, like hair from a wig, or a teddy bear. Except teddy bears smell a lot better."

Her thoughts were broken by a loud, flapping sound. She looked up and saw a big, brown bird with a white head hovering overhead. Its wide, white-tipped wings beat slowly.

"A bald eagle!" Carolyn cried.

"Wow!" the others gasped. Soon all of their cameras were clicking.

The eagle flapped once more and flew away.

While they were still oohing and aahing over the sight, they heard something else nearby. It sounded like a hiss. Or a whisper.

Janet's eyes darted around. "What was that?"

But Barbie was smiling happily. "I'll bet

that's Aspen Falls," she said. "We're almost at our campsite!"

They soon arrived at the falls. Tall, slender aspen trees framed a waterfall formed by three streams. The streams foamed into a deep, inviting blue-green pool.

The hikers spread out their blanket and knelt at the edge of the pool. They splashed their hot faces with cool water. It felt wonderful. The hikers relaxed as they took in the beautiful view of the falls.

"Let's pitch our tents before it gets dark," suggested Barbie a little while later.

They carried their backpacks to a nearby spot where the ground was level. But, as before, someone had been there first.

Or *something*.

"Here we go again," Carolyn murmured.

Broken twigs lay scattered on the ground. Leaves had been flung into ragged piles. The earth was all torn up.

"It looks as if a tornado hit," said Barbie.

"A fur tornado," Carolyn added slowly.

Then everyone noticed the clumps of reddish brown fur everywhere. A strong breeze blew the **unmistakable** sour odor right at them.

Stacie made a gagging sound. Janet clutched her mother's hand. Katie's mouth opened in horror. She was pointing at something behind Barbie.

Barbie wheeled around. Something was hanging from a twig. Something bright orange.

Barbie walked over and carefully took it down, using a plastic bag as a glove again. She held it by one corner.

It was an orange bandanna.

Orange—except for an ugly red stain.

"Blood," Janet whispered. "It's blood. Clawman got the hiker!"

Chapter Four

Carolyn frowned. "I hate to say it, Barbie, but I'm getting worried myself. Maybe we should turn back."

Barbie was concerned, too, and worried about the condition of the missing hiker. But she knew they couldn't turn back.

"Hiking at night in this wilderness would be extremely dangerous," Barbie said. "No, let's set up camp now, while it's still light. Then I'll try to call the ranger station."

Everyone got busy. They pitched the tents and unrolled their mats and sleeping bags. They carried water from the pool and set up for dinner on a flat rock. The girls stayed close together the whole time, not saying a word.

Carolyn cooked a delicious one-pot meal of chicken, vegetables, and rice. But nobody felt much like eating.

Then Barbie tried the ranger station on her phone. "No answer," she reported. "They must still be out searching for the hiker. But I left a message describing what we've found."

The sun dropped below the ridge. Darkness came on quickly. Stars as bright as diamonds speckled the sky.

Barbie pointed out the Milky Way and some **constellations** to calm the girls. But they were too scared to enjoy stargazing. They only wanted to get inside their tent and hide.

"I'm going to keep my flashlight on all night to scare Clawman away," Janet announced.

"Okay, Honey," her mom replied. "Just try to

get some sleep." Carolyn yawned as she crawled into the other tent.

"And remember, our tent is right next to yours," Barbie called. "You're all perfectly safe."

As the others settled in for the night, Barbie examined the orange bandanna. She took careful note of the color of the stain. She flipped through her field guide, marking certain pages with twigs.

Inside the girls' tent, Janet was asleep. She dreamed she was on a train heading up a mountain track. The train's whistle blew. It blew again. The engine turned into Randy's face. The face made a noise like . . .

"Clawman!" she cried out loud.

Janet sat upright in her sleeping bag. The tent was pitch black. Her flashlight batteries were dead. And in the darkness, she heard the dreaded noise again.

"*Woo—EEEE—ah!*"

This was no dream!

"Mom! Barbie! Help!" Janet hollered. "Clawman's coming!"

The noise woke Katie and Stacie. All three girls dived down into their sleeping bags, shaking with fear.

Barbie and Carolyn rushed into the girls' tent. *"Woo—EEEE—ah!"*

The weird howl ripped through the night once more.

"It's Clawman! Don't let him get us!" Katie sobbed.

Janet clung to her mother. "Like he got the hiker!" she cried.

Chapter Five

Barbie and Carolyn moved their sleeping bags into the girls' tent. The five campers spent a restless night crowded together. They didn't hear the strange call again. Still, everyone was glad when daybreak came.

Barbie mixed up chocolate breakfast shakes and passed out granola bars. As they broke down their camp and packed up, something rustled in the bushes. Everyone stood perfectly still.

A tall figure came out of the woods and approached the campsite.

"Morning!" called Ken. "Everyone okay?"

"We're fine," Barbie answered, relieved. "Did you find the hiker?"

"No," he replied. "By now we've covered almost the whole park. The other rangers are on their way. I headed over early to check on you after I got your message. What's going on?"

They took turns describing the previous day's events. Then Barbie opened up the plastic bag with the fur pieces and the bandanna.

"The bandanna matches the description of the one Chris Wilson was wearing," Ken said. "But as for that fur, it's not from any animal I've ever seen. He sniffed and then made a face. "Or smelled!"

"*Now* do you believe it's Clawman?" asked Katie. Freckles stood out on her pale, scared face.

"No," Ken replied, "I still don't believe it is."

"But what about the howling we heard last night?" Stacie protested.

"I don't know what keeps making that sound,' Barbie said. "But as for what's on the bandanna, I doubt that it's blood."

She turned to a marked section of her field guide. It showed pictures of edible plants. "I think what's on the bandanna may be crushed berries or **chokecherries.** And that may be a good sign. It may mean that the hiker has been able to find something to eat."

"But we still don't know what happened to him," Janet said.

"Or why we keep finding places so messed up," Katie added.

"Not yet," said Barbie. "But maybe we'll spot something from up in the fire tower. Meanwhile, let's hope for the best and get to the pond. We have a date with some bald eagles, remember?"

Barbie and Ken led the way down the old

logging road. Behind them, Carolyn and the girls checked their cameras to see how much film they had left. Before long, they saw Eagle Pond. The fire tower loomed high above them. Stairs wound through the center of the tower.

"I'll go up first and check things out," Ken said. He quickly climbed the stairs. A moment later, he appeared at the top and gave a thumbs-up.

Janet's mom went up first. Janet and Katie followed after her. Barbie gave each girl a boost and then turned to help Stacie.

But Stacie had disappeared! Barbie tried not to panic. "Stacie, where are you?" she called. She shaded her eyes and scanned the area.

"She's over there, Barbie," Ken called from the tower. "By the pond."

Barbie glimpsed Stacie's blond hair as her sister skipped around the small body of water. She hurried after her.

Barbie crossed a large snowy spot. She saw

more tracks in the snow. Some of them were like the ones from the trail. But the last cluster was very big. The three points formed a triangle.

"Three points, three claws," Barbie thought. Her heart started to hammer. "I *know* Clawman isn't real. But still . . . Stacie!" she called. "Come back!"

Her little sister waved and started walking toward her.

Barbie studied the tracks again. Its three points were so far apart. Much too far apart to have been made by any animal or bird. At least by any *ordinary* animal or bird.

Then she heard that familiar, terrifying sound. *"Woo—EEEE—ah!"*

Something crashed and pounded in the narrow strip of woods next to the pond. The wind carried that same sickly odor.

Barbie was taking no chances. "Stacie, run!"

But Stacie was already on her way. She raced away from the woods and threw herself into Barbie's arms. Barbie swept her into a big hug.

"Woo—EEEE—ah!"

Barbie was determined to get to the bottom o this mystery once and for all.

Clutching Stacie tightly, she raised her binoculars toward the thin strip of woods. What sh saw made her gasp.

She lowered the binoculars and rubbed her eyes. Then she adjusted the focus and looked again. "I don't believe it!" she exclaimed.

"Believe what?" Stacie asked. "Is it Clawmar

They heard a commotion up in the fire tower. Barbie looked up to see Ken frantically motioning to her to come up.

Katie and Janet pointed to the woods, yelling "Clawman!"

Carolyn shouted, "Run! Run!"

Chapter Six

Stacie whimpered.

"Don't worry, Sweetie," Barbie told her. "It's okay. But let's get you up to the tower."

Ken charged down the stairs. His face was tight with concern. Stacie raced up the winding stairs. Carolyn reached down and pulled her up to the top.

"Aren't you coming?" she called to Barbie.

"No," Barbie answered. "Not yet. We've got something to do. But don't worry!"

She grabbed Ken's hand. "Come on!" she said. "You have to see something! You simply

39

won't believe it!"

"But I just *did* see something!" Ken replied in alarm. "I saw Clawman, right in those woods. I guess he *is* real! That's why I was yelling for you to come up."

"No," Barbie said. "What you saw was not Clawman. Unless Clawman wears sneakers!"

Ken was totally puzzled. "Sneakers?"

"Through my binoculars, I saw a tall figure with fur all over. Something like a bear's head covered its face. But I'm not kidding—it had on high-tops! And now I remember seeing footprints next to those tracks we saw in the snow."

Ken was silent for a moment. Then he sighed "I don't get it, but I trust you, Barbie. Let's go see what's up!"

They trotted around the pond. Pushing aside prickly branches, they tiptoed into the bushes.

They were quiet, but the tall, furry creature hiding there heard them anyway.

It turned its big bear's head and looked straight at them. Barbie held back a shudder. It looked just like the famous picture of Clawman from books and TV.

The creature began to run.

"Stop!" Barbie called. "Come back!"

The creature kept looking back over its shoulder as it ran. Finally it stumbled and fell over a fallen tree limb.

Barbie and Ken hurried over.

Ken's jaw dropped. "What in the world?"

Sitting there, holding his ankle, was a young man. A bear's-head mask had been pushed up off his face. His body was covered with brownish red, ratty-looking fur.

A camera dangled from his neck. A photographer's **tripod** lay next to him. Its three legs were closed. But when opened, they would look like three giant, widely spaced claws.

The young man wore black high-tops. His

41

hands were stained red. And he smelled *terrible!*

"Clawman, I presume?" Barbie asked, arms folded across her chest.

"Actually, I'm Chris Wilson," answered the ridiculous-looking creature.

"Chris Wilson!" exclaimed Ken. "The hiker! We've been searching for you!"

"And it looks as if *we've* been following you," Barbie said. "Not on purpose, I might add."

Chris pulled the bear mask off his head. "I'm sorry," he said. "I never meant to cause any trouble. I should have known my buddies wouldn't trust my wilderness skills and would call the ranger."

Carolyn, Janet, Katie, and Stacie had seen the chase from the tower. Now they joined Barbie and Ken, keeping their distance from the smelly Chris Wilson.

"Want to tell us what's going on?" Barbie asked Chris.

Still rubbing his ankle, Chris slowly stood up. Under all the dirt, his face was a mass of insect bites. He scratched at them as he told his story.

"I'm a photographer. I was at the Johnson city newspaper earlier this week, trying to sell some pictures. I overheard someone call with a hot tip: Clawman had been sighted at Eagle Pond! The caller wanted money for the information, but the editor said she would only pay for a picture. So I decided to take some."

Chris moved a little closer. The group moved a little farther away.

"So why the costume?" Carolyn asked.

Chris replied, "I read that long ago, hunters would dress up in buffalo skins. That way they could get closer to the buffalo herd. So I bought an old fake-fur coat at a junk store and turned it into a bodysuit. I made a bear's head mask out of **papier-mâché** and painted it. Then I mixed fish oil and other stuff to match Clawman's smell."

The girls wrinkled their noses and moved even farther away.

"Then I hiked into the woods and started acting like Clawman, trying to get him to come out," Chris continued. "I made lots of noise and imitated his cry and left clumps of fur all over the place. I even collected chokecherries in my bandanna, because I'd heard that's what he liked to eat. But I lost it somewhere."

"We found it," said Barbie. "But how did you know what Clawman was supposed to sound like?"

"From the person with the tip. He made such a loud Clawman call that I could hear it clear across the editor's office," Chris explained.

"Randy," Carolyn whispered.

Barbie and Ken nodded.

Chris looked down at the ground. "The tip must have been phony, because Clawman never showed up. But I found such unbelievable scenery that I used up almost all my film taking nature shots."

Barbie fished out the piece of black plastic she had found. "So this was your lens cap," she said. "And the tracks we saw were made by your tripod?"

"Right," Chris admitted. "I folded up the legs and used it for balance, like a walking stick."

Barbie continued. "That's why the points were so close together. The last track I saw, with

three holes spread out, must have been made when you opened up the tripod to shoot.

"Right again," Chris replied

Janet spoke up timidly. "Now that we know we don't have to be scared anymore, will you show us how you made the Clawman sound?"

Chris puckered his lips and threw his head

back. *"Woo—EEEE—ah!"*

The girls covered their ears and laughed.

Suddenly there was another sound. It was a loud, flapping noise.

They ran to see a pair of bald eagles flying over the pond. The magnificent birds swooped down to the water. They came back up holding silver-scaled fish in their beaks.

Excitedly, Janet's mom and the girls snapped the last of their pictures. So did Chris.

But something interrupted them.

"Woo—EEEE—ah!"

"Who did that?" cried Barbie, turning toward the noise.

"Now's my chance!" Chris shouted. "I've finally found Clawman! Or he's found me!"

He rushed back into the woods.

Chapter Seven

"Woo—EEEE—ah! Woo—EEEE—ah!"

The sounds came one after another, and with them, all the girls' worst fears came rushing back.

"Clawman *is* real!" Janet cried. "Let's go hide in the tower!"

"Barbie, I think Janet's right," said Carolyn. "Let's go!"

But Barbie stayed calm. She looked through her binoculars at a pine tree. Then she smiled. "No need to panic," she reported. "A little birdie just told me there's nothing to worry about."

Slowly Chris rejoined the group. His

shoulders were slumped in disappointment. "I'm out of film! Just when I might have had the real Clawman and made some big money."

"There is no real Clawman," Barbie replied. "There was only you and another talented imitator."

A gray-and-white mockingbird flew out of a pine tree. He shrilled *"Woo—EEEE—ah!"* over and over. Then he flew away.

Everything became quiet for a moment.

"Well, you certainly solved the mystery, Barbie," said Carolyn, laughing. "Good job!"

"And I *did* get some great nature shots," Chris added. "Maybe the editor will buy them instead of Clawman pictures. I'll stop by her office when we get to town."

Ken put his walkie-talkie away. "I talked to the search party," he reported. "I told them we had found our missing hiker and that we could use a lift to town. They'll meet us in jeeps down the road."

Barbie took a large, folded garbage bag from her backpack. "Before we all travel together, Chris, why don't you get rid of Clawman's—er, personality?"

Chris wriggled out of the costume and dropped it in the bag. Then he added the headpiece. "I guess I won't be needing these anymore."

"No, but you will need a bath," said Carolyn as the girls giggled.

On the way back to town, Chris apologized to everyone. "I didn't mean to mess up your trip or mess up the woods, either. Guess I wasn't thinking of anything but getting those pictures."

The photographer looked miserable. Barbie knew that he wished he had never heard of Clawman. As they dropped him off in town, Barbie patted his arm and wished him luck. She had a feeling that from now on, Chris would choose the nature he photographed more carefully.

Everyone slept soundly that night. The next

day, they packed and waited on the porch for Ken to take them to the airport.

Randy approached them, beaming.

"I'm sure glad to see you're all safe and sound," Randy said, "because it turns out Clawman really is on the loose!"

"Oh?" Barbie asked. "How can you be sure?"

"I know it for a fact," he replied. "See, I wanted to find Clawman myself. So I went out into the woods after you. I found pieces of stinko fur everywhere, so I knew he had to be out there. Finally I heard his cry. You know, the one that goes—"

"We know," Carolyn and the girls interrupted. "You don't need to show us."

"I followed the sound, and I saw him," Randy continued. "I didn't get too close, but close enough for a darn good picture." He winked at them. "The best part is, I know someone who

will pay me a ton of money for it!"

Barbie's eyes twinkled. "Oh, really?" she said. "Even for a picture of Clawman wearing sneakers?"

Randy was puzzled. "Clawman doesn't wear sneakers! What are you talking about?"

"Take a look at your photo," Barbie said.

Randy pulled out the picture. The girls crowded around. There was Chris Wilson in his Clawman costume, complete with black high-tops. They clapped their hands over their mouths to hold back their giggles.

Randy was shocked. "How did you know Clawman wears sneakers?" he asked Barbie.

"Let's just say we got a hot tip," Barbie told him. She winked at the others as they waved good-bye to Randy. It was time to go home.